WELCOME TO

Beast Quest

Collect the special coins in this book.
You will earn one gold coin for
every chapter you read.

Once you have finished all the chapters,
find out what to do with your gold coins at
the back of the book.

With special thanks to Tabitha Jones

For Moxley O'Neill

www.beastquest.co.uk

ORCHARD BOOKS
Carmelite House
50 Victoria Embankment
London EC4Y 0DZ

A Paperback Original
First published in Great Britain in 2015

Beast Quest is a registered trademark of Beast Quest Limited
Series created by Beast Quest Limited, London

Text © Beast Quest Limited 2015
Cover and inside illustrations by Steve Sims
© Beast Quest Limited 2015

A CIP catalogue record for this book is available from
the British Library.

ISBN 978 1 40833 988 6

1 3 5 7 9 10 8 6 4 2

Printed and bound by CPI Group (UK) Ltd, Croydon, CR0 4YY

MIX
Paper from
responsible sources
FSC www.fsc.org **FSC® C104740**

The paper and board used in this book are made from wood
from responsible sources.

Orchard Books
An imprint of Hachette Children's Group
Part of The Watts Publishing Group Limited
An Hachette UK company

www.hachette.co.uk

SOLIX
THE DEADLY SWARM

BY ADAM BLADE

ORCHARD

THE ICE
CASTLE

CRESCENT CAVE

FREESHOR

CITY OF
JENGTOR

Fe

GWILDORIAN
PLAINS

THE RAINBOW JUNGL

GWILDOR

ION

GWILDORIAN OCEAN

LAND

FISHING
VILLAGE

CONTENTS

Greetings, followers of the Quest,

I am Irina, the Good Witch of Avantia's twin kingdom, Gwildor. This was supposed to be a time of happiness, as we welcomed young heroes Tom and Elenna to our capital city Jengtor. Freya, Tom's mother and Mistress of the Beasts, beamed with pride at the thought of her son's arrival.

She smiles no longer.

Someone else has been awaiting Tom's arrival. We should have known our enemies would choose this moment to strike. Now Freya lies in my chamber, unable to command her Beasts. And Jengtor is under siege from a deadly menace that attacks from the skies.

Our only hope lies with Tom and Elenna, but they are walking right into a trap.

Irina, loyal Witch of Gwildor

A STRANGER IN NEED

Tom leaned low over Angel's neck, the thud of galloping hooves jolting though his tense muscles. At his side, Elenna rode Star, her short hair tugged back by the wind.

The bright Gwildorian sky arched high above them, a cloudless blaze of sapphire blue, and rolling grassland swept by on either side. But Tom's mind's eye was turned inwards to an image of his mother, sick from an evil poison. She lay in Jengtor, the Gwildorian capital, which was under attack from the Pirate King, Sanpao. Only the Good Witch Irina's magical force field protected the citizens from Sanpao's barrage of cannon fire – and the force field was being eaten away day by day, moment by moment. Tom scanned the flat horizon, and took a deep breath, trying to control the emotions raging inside him. He and Elenna were still at least two days' ride from Jengtor. *We have to get there in time!*

Angel's hooves barely seemed to touch the ground as she flew over the grassy plains. The rushing wind cooled Tom's face, and with the release of speed, his spirits lifted. *If we keep going at this pace, we'll make up for the time we've lost defeating Kensa's enchanted Beasts.* Sanpao's witch companion had created a magical potion that could turn ordinary creatures into deadly monsters. Tom and Elenna had already battled two since their arrival in Gwildor.

Tom squinted into the sun and noticed a dark spot streaking towards them through the sky. He called on the enhanced vision from his golden helmet, and saw at once that it was a sleek blue dove carrying a vial in its beak.

"A royal messenger from Jengtor!" he called to Elenna, tugging on the reins to bring Angel to a stop, as the bird let the tiny vial fall. Tom snatched the vial from the air.

Elenna pulled up beside him, her brows pinched together with concern. "I hope it's good news this time," she said.

Tom gritted his teeth, his chest tight with worry as he pulled the stopper from the vial. It released billowing purple smoke, which spread to form a swirling cloud. Then the vapour at the centre of the

cloud thinned, forming an image of
elegant spires and graceful bridges
beneath a shimmering dome of light.
Irina's force field, Tom realised.

The Good Witch had told him she had conjured a magical shield to protect Jengtor from the pirates.

But the dark shape of Sanpao's flying ship was hovering over the dome, black cannon jutting from its portholes. *No!* Tom's belly churned with dread as the cannon fired a volley of missiles towards the city. The force field flared bright where the cannonballs hit, and then burned dimmer and paler once they had tumbled away.

"Irina's magic is weakening," Elenna said.

Tom gripped the hilt of his sword. "I'm going to make Sanpao pay!" he said. Frustration burned in his chest as he thought of the distance they still had to travel. *I wish I had the power to step inside that vision!*

The magical image before him shifted suddenly. The viewpoint swept downwards through Irina's force field, over the broad, mansion-lined streets of Jengtor, and into the gilded palace at the heart of the city.

Tom felt his heart clench.

"Oh!" Elenna gasped. Tom's mother, Freya, lay in a four-poster bed, half hidden by richly patterned curtains. At her side, Irina leaned forward to press a damp cloth to Freya's pale brow. Freya frowned and lifted her arm, pushing Irina's hand away. Tom felt a glimmer of hope as his mother's eyes flickered open – but there was no recognition in her misty, wide-eyed stare.

Irina stood back from the bed and turned to gaze out through the veil of purple smoke. Tom was shocked by how changed she was. Her eyes were filled with sorrow, and there were dark circles beneath them that hadn't been there before.

"Tom and Elenna," Irina's voice said. Tom leaned forward, straining to hear her words over the muffled crash and thud of cannon. "I can only hope you receive this message," Irina continued. "Time is running out, and I fear that without your help, all will be lost. You must reach Jengtor soon…"

The purple smoke swirled and started to drift.

"Irina! Wait!" Tom cried, but the vision wavered, shifted out of focus and dissolved.

As Tom watched the purple tendrils of smoke drift up into the azure sky, cold horror gripped hold of him, chilling him to the bones. Elenna turned towards him, and Tom could see his own fears mirrored in her expression.

"Use your magic horseshoe to go ahead," she said. "I will follow as quickly as I can."

Tom rubbed his hands over his face. "I don't want to leave you alone with Kensa and Sanpao on the loose," he said. "But I don't think we have a choice."

"Go!" Elenna insisted. "Your mother needs you."

"Be careful," said Tom. Then he turned and put his heels to Angel's sides.

The mare's sleek muscles bunched beneath him as she sprang into a gallop. Tom put his hand to the horseshoe fragment in his shield, and called on its magical speed. His stomach lurched as Angel surged forwards, racing over the grassland as smoothly and as swiftly as the wind. The bright landscape flashed by in a blur of greens and golds.

But then a desperate cry cut through the swish of the wind. Tom sat back and tugged at the reins, and Angel thundered to a stop. Tom turned his head, listening hard.

The cry came again, and this time he could hear it clearly. "Tom! I need you!"

Elenna!

Tom called on the magic eyesight from his golden helmet. He gazed back the way he had come, scanning the swaying grasses. A dark shape caught his eye, and he focussed in on it. Elenna was bent low

beside her horse, staring intently at a shadow in the grass. As Tom watched, she leaned down and lifted something, cradling it in her arms. Long dark hair fell back from a young girl's face, streaked with dirt.

Her eyes were closed.

"I'm coming, Elenna!" Tom shouted.

EVIL IN THE JUNGLE

Tom swung down from the saddle and landed beside his friend.

Elenna was sitting in the grass, supporting the dark-haired girl's head with one arm. She looked to be no older than six.

"She was just lying by the side of the road!" Elenna said. "I can't wake her."

Tom bent over the girl. Her
skin was tanned but there was no
warmth to her colour at all, as if all
her blood had drained away. Her
forehead was slick with sweat, and
huge red spots covered her face and

arms, oozing grey pus. Tom winced
at the sight of them.

Elenna put her flask to the girl's
parched lips but the water trickled
out of her mouth onto the ground.
"She needs to drink something,"

Elenna said. "She's burning up."

Tom sank to his knees beside the girl and tugged Epos's healing talon from his shield. He held it near one of the spots, and watched with relief as the spot shrank away, the redness around it fading. Tom passed the talon over the rest of the girl's body. The spots quickly healed, and her skin took on a healthier tone. As Elenna brushed the damp hair back from the girl's face, her eyes fluttered open.

"No! Get away!" she cried, squirming from Elenna's grasp and scrambling to her feet. She ran a few unsteady paces.

"Wait!" Tom said. "We mean

you no harm!"

The girl turned and frowned, shading her eyes. She was slight, and dressed in a simple orange tunic. Her legs and feet were bare. A look of panic crossed her face as she scanned the empty grassland around her.

"Where am I?" she said. "This isn't the jungle!"

"You are in farmland," Elenna told her, "some way from the Rainbow Jungle. We found you lying by the side of the road. You've been very sick."

"I can't remember walking here..." the girl said, putting her hand to her head. "We were attacked!"

A stab of worry jolted along Tom's spine. Could this be Sanpao's doing? Or Kensa and her enchanted Beasts?

"I was bitten and stung..." the girl went on, shuddering. Elenna put an arm across her shoulders.

"What sort of animal stung you?" Tom asked.

"Ants," the girl said. "So many ants!" She shuddered again, and brushed at her skin with her hands as if she could still feel tiny legs crawling all over her.

"Tell us from the beginning," Elenna said gently.

The girl took a shaky breath, then nodded. "My name is Orla," she said. "My home lies deep inside the Rainbow Jungle. My tribe have always lived in harmony with the creatures there, and the ants were our friends. But recently, the ants started spoiling food and damaging plants. And one night, they came to the village and attacked. The elders tried to drive them away with fiddles and drums, but they just kept coming back... There are so many of them."

The girl stopped, twisting the hem of her tunic in her hands, staring into the distance. "The village had only just recovered from the pirate raids, we couldn't defend ourselves."

"Pirates?" Tom asked.

Orla wrinkled her nose. "They're

horrible," she said. "Big, smelly men with cruel weapons. They threaten the elders and steal whatever takes their fancy."

Fury burned in Tom's belly, flowing hot through his veins.

"Sanpao," Elenna said. "His men must be marauding all over Gwildor!"

"I have to get home!" Orla cried. "Mother will be so worried!"

Elenna handed the girl her water flask. "Drink this," she said. "You will need to gather your strength before you can travel."

"Thank you," Orla said, taking the flask in shaking hands and putting it to her lips.

As the young girl drank, Tom beckoned Elenna aside. "We can't leave Orla here alone," he said, "and my gut tells me this could be Kensa's doing. We'll take Orla back to her people, and offer what help we can, but we must be quick. We have to reach Jengtor soon, or lives will be lost."

Elenna nodded. "Orla can ride with me. If we travel fast, we shouldn't lose too much time."

Tom and Elenna turned back to Orla. She was gazing south, gnawing at her lip.

"We'll ride with you back to the jungle," Elenna said. "We'll help you find your people."

"Thank you!" Orla cried, throwing her arms around Elenna.

Once the girl had let go, Elenna swung onto Star's back. Tom lifted Orla up behind her, then leapt into Angel's saddle. They started off towards the southern horizon at a gallop.

Soon, the darker deeper green of the Rainbow Jungle rose up before them.

"There!" yelled Orla, looking happy to see her home.

Tom eased Angel to a trot. Elenna did the same.

As they approached the treeline, Tom leapt from Angel's back. He reached into her saddlebag and took

out the ram's horn he'd won during
his battle against Ronak, tucking it
into his belt.

Tokens won from Beast battles

have a habit of coming in handy...

Elenna swung from Star's saddle, and put out a hand to help Orla down.

"We'll be back soon," Tom said, running his hand down Angel's soft nose. The horse raised her head and whickered, then lowered it to the ground and started nibbling at the grass.

Tom turned towards the leafy shadows of the Rainbow Jungle. He could hear muted hoots and croaks from the canopy above and the rustle of small creatures roaming the jungle floor. Orla was already striding ahead towards the undergrowth. Tom took a deep breath and squared his shoulders. Somewhere in the darkness ahead, another of Kensa's Evil Beasts could be waiting.

I just hope we're ready for it!

FLESH-EATING ANTS

"Tread where I tread..." Orla looked back at Tom and Elenna from the leafy shadows at the edge of the jungle. "Many of the plants are so poisonous that even touching them can be deadly," she warned.

Tom and Elenna exchanged an uneasy look. They'd been in this jungle before and knew Orla wasn't exaggerating.

As Tom stepped into the jungle behind Orla, stifling, muggy heat hit him like a giant, clammy hand. The smell of lush vegetation and rotting leaves hung thick in the air, and a warm mist rose up from the dark earth all around him. Through the hazy gloom, shiny flowers glowed bright in rich, vibrant colours.

Tom did his best to put his boots where Orla's bare feet trod. He moved slowly, careful not to touch the snaking vines hanging from above. A twig cracked under his heel, and a startled bird flapped across their path with a flurry of rainbow wings.

Orla turned to him, a finger to

her lips. "We don't want to draw
the ants." She pressed on. Tom
marvelled at her ability to move

silently, almost effortlessly, through the dense undergrowth. He could hear Elenna behind him, panting in the heat, and his own tunic clung to his back, damp with sweat.

As they trudged on, Tom noticed ferns with broken stems littering their path alongside crushed flowers, and browning leaves covered with a strange, grey slime.

"What is that stuff?" Elenna asked, wrinkling her nose at a dripping leaf.

Orla glanced back. "It's from the ants," she said. "Normally, they help us by clearing away the dangerous plants. But recently they've started killing everything. Just look." She lifted a huge, lacy fern. The edge was crinkled and dry, and showed a line of ragged bite-marks. "They've been taking plants deep into the jungle, and what they don't take, they destroy."

The further they travelled, the more plants showed signs of damage.

Finally Orla stopped and turned, her eyes bright in the gloom.

"My village is just through here," she said, gesturing to a curtain of hanging vines. She ducked through the creepers. Tom and Elenna pushed through the vines behind her, into a circular clearing, lined with small huts that were thatched

with leaves. Many of them had been
flattened, and wooden bowls and
pots lay scattered on the ground,
alongside drums and carved fiddles.
A circle of blackened earth ringed
by stones showed where the village

fire had burned. An extinguished torch lay on the ground outside the largest hut, and the earth in the centre of the clearing was scuffed.

Orla fell to her knees with a gasp. "What's happened?"

Tom crossed to the disturbed patch of earth. He saw human footprints, and the tiny pin-prick marks of insects. He felt a shiver pass down his spine. Apart from the small sounds of the jungle, the village was silent. Tom picked up the torch and tucked it under his arm.

This might come in useful.

"Where is everyone?" Orla said, her voice choked with tears. "Perhaps they ran to safety?"

Elenna put her hand on Orla's shoulder. "We'll help you find them," she promised.

"And while there's blood in my veins, we'll defeat whatever did this to your village," Tom vowed.

Suddenly Elenna let out a gasp and darted across the clearing. "Look!" she cried.

Tom raced to her side, and his guts churned. Poking from the moss at the edge of the clearing, he could see a line of pointed ribs. Then he noticed the bony ridge of an eye socket protruding from a skull. It was the skeleton of some animal – a goat or a lamb – picked almost clean of flesh. Orla buried her face in Elenna's tunic. Tom shook his head in horror.

"How many ants would it take to do this?" he said. "And…why are they doing it?"

Orla peeked around Elenna into the dark trees surrounding the clearing. "I don't understand," she said. "The ants have always been our allies. We protected their homes. But then they turned black, and started destroying things and—" Orla stopped speaking and gasped, wide-eyed with fear.

A horrible, scrabbling scratching was coming from the jungle ahead…

The sound was building by the moment. It made Tom's scalp tingle

with fear. *It's only ants,* he reminded himself. *Tiny insects.* But then he thought of the skeleton, picked clean. He'd seen something like this before.

Creta the Winged Terror had been made of a swarm of vicious Stabiors.

Insects can be deadly.

Tom and Elenna peered into the dense undergrowth, looking for the source of the rustling. Then Tom froze. A shiny black stream of scurrying insects began to flow from the treeline, spreading like spilled ink, straight towards them.

4

EATEN ALIVE

"We must get out of here!" Orla cried. "But move slowly. The ants can't see much, but they hear everything."

Tom held his breath, his eyes on the advancing army of insects as he, Elenna and Orla backed slowly into the trees at the edge of the village. Tom watched as broken branches

and huge, slime-covered leaves
emerged from the shadows on the
other side of the clearing, held up
by countless tiny black ants.

They seemed to have gathered
enough food for half of Gwildor,
Tom thought. *But where are they*

taking it? He glanced at the small, frightened girl at his side and thought of the missing villagers... the animal skeleton.

They're taking it to a Beast...

The heavily laden troupe of ants marched steadily through the

clearing, and slowly disappeared into the deep shadows of the jungle beyond.

"Let's follow them," Tom said.

Orla led the way into the thick undergrowth, taking a path parallel to the ants. Tom and Elenna followed her through the stifling half-darkness, listening to the hideous scratching sound of the marching ants. Each time Tom caught a new glimpse of the creatures, they seem to have picked up even more vegetation, until they looked like a flowing river, choked with wood and leaves.

They came to a stagnant pond, clogged with stringy weed.

As they skirted round it, Tom's feet
sank deep into the boggy ground,
sending noxious gasses bubbling up
from the mud. Elenna winced and
covered her nose with her hand. Tom
hoped the ants couldn't hear the
squelching of their boots.

At last they moved past the boggy
ground as Orla led them onwards,
into even thicker undergrowth.
Soon, the rustle of the ants tramping
through the leaf litter sounded
muffled in the heavy air. Elenna
pointed to her ear. Tom realised he
couldn't hear a single bird or animal
calling. *Even the jungle creatures
are afraid,* he thought.

Crack! A twig snapped under

Tom's boot, cutting the silence. He froze, his breath caught in his throat. Had the ants heard? Tom's heart hammered. The rustling had stopped. Orla leaned forwards, worriedly, peering into the gloom. Tom could just make out the blot of deeper darkness in the shadows.

A high-pitched click sounded from the river of ants. Then another. A faint shimmer ran through the carpet of creatures as they all turned at once. Then the tide began to move again, but now it was heading straight towards Tom, Elenna and Orla.

Tom swallowed hard, his pulse thrashing in his ears. "They're coming for us!" He glanced about the shadows, looking for a way out.

"Those ants can eat through flesh!" Elenna hissed. "We have to get out of their path."

"Run!" Tom cried, pointing towards a narrow gap in the undergrowth. Elenna took Orla's hand and raced away.

Tom plunged through the trees behind them, his pace slowing when he heard the faint, scrabbling sound of the ants ahead of them, as well as behind. Elenna darted away to the left, taking Orla with her. Tom followed, but before long they were met with another angry flurry of clicking.

The ants were heading them off!

We'll never escape in the deadly undergrowth, Tom realised. *But maybe we can scare the ants away!*

"Orla, Elenna, get behind me!" Tom hissed.

"What are you going to do?" Elenna asked.

"I'm going to start a fire."

Tom handed Elenna the torch he was carrying, and dropped to his knees, tugging his flint from his pouch. He snatched up a rotting branch and scraped at the wood until he had a pile of soft, white splinters. Then, he held his flint above the pile and struck the smooth stone hard with his sword.

A tiny spark flew. It landed on the wood but quickly burned out. Tom's spine was tingling at the hideous clamour of the advancing ants. He

tried to put the sound from
his mind.

"Hurry!" Elenna hissed. "They're
coming."

Tom smashed the blade against
the flint once more. A bright spark
flew, and landed on the wood. Tom
leaned forwards, and blew softly,
willing the spark to catch. There
was a flare of orange, and the wood
chips fizzled. Tom glanced over his
shoulder, to see the ants almost
at his heels. He cupped his hands
around his tiny fire.

"Now!" he told Elenna. She
thrust the tip of her torch into the
small flames. The oil-steeped tip
caught alight, and Elenna stepped

back with Orla behind her. Tom lurched to his feet as Elenna waved the burning torch. Tom felt a maddening tickle at his knee.

Orla screamed, pointing a shaking finger at Tom's leg. He looked down to see ants pouring over him, clambering into his boots, scurrying inside his clothes. He felt stabs of pain in his ankle, and at the back of his knee. An image of the animal skeleton flashed through his mind and his heart leapt with panic.

I'm being eaten alive!

A DESPERATE PLUNGE

Elenna jumped past Tom, holding her torch low to the ground. She swung it from side to side, forcing the advancing ants back with the flame.

Tom could feel the insects climbing up his body. He hopped from foot to foot, slapping

frantically at his skin, but he could
already feel the ants under his
tunic, climbing his neck!

Elenna turned and thrust the tip

of her torch towards him. Tom's
heart clenched with horror.

"No!" he said. "If you make them
panic, they'll bite!"

"But we have to get them off you!"
Elenna cried.

More insects were swarming up
Tom's body, biting at his chest and
neck, climbing into his ears and
crawling through his hair. He took
a shuddering breath, trying to think
through the agony and panic…

The pool!

"Follow me!" he cried.

"Where are we going? We need to
get those things off you!" Elenna
shouted. But Tom couldn't answer.
He could feel ants at the corners of

his mouth, trying to crawl in. He pressed his lips tightly together, turned and ran.

Tom raced back along the path they had followed, leaping over gnarled roots and crashing through vines and ferns, the jungle a blur of shadows on either side. Branches whipped his face and snatched at his clothes. Everywhere, sharp jaws jabbed his skin. He thought he was going to faint from the searing pain.

Finally, he burst headlong through a wall of vegetation to find the putrid pool before him. He bent his legs, took a deep breath and hurled himself into the water.

Rotting lily pads parted around

him as he plunged into the murky pool. Soft, gooey mud and matted weeds met his outstretched fingers, and bubbles and silt rose up before his eyes. Tom thrashed, scraping at his skin and clothes with his hands. Before long, his lungs were burning for air but he forced himself to stay under, until the ants were all gone.

Finally, when his whole body was screaming for air, he heaved himself up to standing. Tom pushed his dripping hair back from his face and scraped the mud from his eyes. His clothes were drenched and covered with weed, but he couldn't see any ants. He spat out a glob of mud and blew a stream of rancid water from his nose. Elenna and Orla watched from the edge of the pool, eyes wide with concern.

"Are you all right?" Elenna asked, using the flaming torch to inspect him. Tom looked himself over, relieved to see that the ants appeared to have backed off for now.

Tom waded through the shallow pond to join them on the shore. "I think so," he said. "Are they gone?" He tugged up his tunic.

Elenna held her torch above him, and ran her eyes over his skin. She nodded. "The ants are gone, but you've got a few nasty stings."

Tom looked down to see angry red

welts on his stomach and arms, grey
pimples already forming at their
centres. He let his tunic fall.

"The ants never used to sting,"
Orla said quietly. "Not until they

turned black. They always used to be red."

Tom frowned, thinking of Kensa's evil potions. "There is nothing natural about the way those ants are behaving," he said. "We'd better get after them. These stings won't slow me down." Tom started off into the jungle. He didn't need Orla to lead him now. The ants had left a wide path of bare earth and gnawed, slime-drenched stems. It led them further and further into the dark depths of the jungle. Tom could hardly catch his breath in the steamy heat, and his clothes weren't drying at all.

Beside him, Elenna suddenly

grabbed his sleeve and stopped before a tattered veil of moss hanging from an ancient, twisted tree. She put a finger to her lips. Tom could hear a faint scratching sound coming from up ahead.

"The ants," Orla whispered.

"I'll go first," Tom said, pushing through the pale curtain. A mossy, grey cliff-face rose up before him, half smothered with creeping plants. A broad overhang protruded from the cliff, crumbling away in places. Bright plants peeked from between cracks in mounds of fallen rubble.

Long stalactites hung like gnarled fingers from the lip of the overhang,

and behind them, a dark opening
in the rock stretched away into
blackness. The scraping sound was
coming from inside.

"A cave," Elenna said.

"Or a lair," Tom answered. He crept over the rubble-strewn ground, and stepped beneath the overhang with Orla and Elenna at his back. Shafts of light broke through cracks in the ceiling of the cavern, and ferns and mosses covered the floor. In the centre of the cave, a huge mound of earth reached upwards, tapering to a knobbly peak. It was pitted with holes and shimmered with the movement of thousands of tiny black insects. All around the vast ant hill lay slime-covered flowers and leaves.

Suddenly a blinding red light filled the cave, like the glare of the evening sun. Tom reeled back, shielding his face with arm. The light faded, and Tom blinked as colours pulsed behind his eyes. All he could make out in the dark cave ahead was the shape of the writhing ant hill.

Then something rose up before it – something black and shining and immense.

"What is it?" Orla asked, her words barely more than a squeak. Tom put his hand to the red jewel in his shield, and heard a dry, rasping voice in his mind – a venomous hiss, like the rustle of dead leaves.

What am I? the voice asked. *I am Solix the Deadly Swarm and I will devour your flesh and pick your feeble skeletons clean!*

THE DEADLY SWARM

Dread pulsed through Tom as
he stared at the huge Beast in
the cave. Solix was formed from
millions of tiny ants. The insects
scurried towards her, climbing
the dark shape and adding to her
vast, writhing bulk. Long, jointed
legs appeared as thousands of ants

melded together, growing out from
a segmented body. Her smooth head
was huge, with twitching antennae
and curved pincers covered in

spikes. The Beast was a giant ant, and as she moved, her shell glinted in the light filtering down from the roof of the cave.

"What is it?" Orla whimpered.

"A Beast made of ants," Elenna shouted.

"One of Kensa's enchantments," Tom said. "And somehow, we're going to defeat it."

The echo of their voices sounded off the rock all around them. Solix turned sharply, her long antennae quivering and her pincers opening wide. "Prepare to die."

"Elenna, keep Orla safe," Tom said. His friend shielded the girl behind her body, huddling against the cave wall in a pool of orange torchlight.

Tom drew his sword, and stepped towards the Beast. The giant ant shot forwards, her jaws snapping. Tom leapt back as Solix's jaws clashed together, just a hand's breadth from

his chest. Tom swung his shield sideways, smashing it into the Beast's serrated mandibles with all his strength. Solix hissed, her antennae whipping about. Then she lunged again.

Tom spun, slicing his sword downwards towards the scissor-like mandibles.

His blade slashed through the tip of a pincer, slicing it off. Solix let out a furious hiss and snatched her jaws out of reach, backing deeper into the cave. Tom looked down to see the severed tip of the mandible disintegrate into thousands of black ants. The insects scurried back towards Solix. Tom watched with growing dread as the ants clambered up the Beast's leg and onto her glittering abdomen. Solix's smooth exoskeleton shimmered, and her broken mandible re-formed before Tom's eyes.

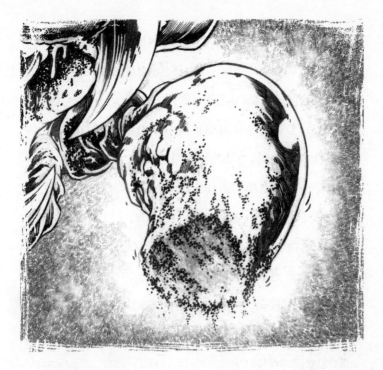

"She can heal herself!" Elenna
cried.

More ants swarmed towards the
giant insect, pouring into the cave
from every crack and crevice. The
Beast grew taller and broader,

swelling to twice her original size.

Tom lifted his blade and started to circle the Beast, his heart pounding against his ribs as he took in the immense size of her bloated body. *How can I defeat something that is indestructible?*

A serrated foreleg lashed towards his face. Tom ducked beneath it and lunged, thrusting the tip of his sword deep into the giant ant's shiny body.

Solix let out a furious sound like steam erupting from a geyser. She reared up, towering over Tom, spiked limbs twitching madly and dark eyes filled with rage. Tom could see that her bulbous abdomen tapered to a needle-sharp point between her back legs. At its tip, Tom could see a drop of milky venom.

A stinger.

He tightened his grip on his sword.

Solix gave a rasping hiss, and a razor-edged limb jabbed towards him.

CRACK! Tom smashed it away with the flat of his blade.

Another jointed limb whipped from the shadows. Tom knocked it aside with his shield.

There was a glint of movement from above him: torchlight shimmering on inky shell. Solix's vast pincers came crashing down. Tom leapt back and lifted his shield. He felt a thump as the blow connected. Then, in a blur of movement almost too fast for Tom to register, a barbed foot sliced towards his face.

"Aargh!" Tom staggered back, clutching his burning cheek. He could feel warm blood on his hand.

"Tom! Look out!" Elenna cried.

Tom saw the gleaming tip of Solix's abdomen stabbing towards him.

He called on the power of his golden boots and sprang. He flew upwards, over Solix's domed head, swiping his sword in an arc beneath his feet.

His blade bit deep into the

creature's skull. Solix let out a rasping hiss of rage. Tom landed behind the Beast and spun to see her lower her body back to the ground, quivering with pain and fury. Her head thrashed from side to side.

A tide of ants scurried over the cave floor and up her legs, joining her trembling body. The wound on her head shimmered and closed, but still more ants came. Tom watched in horror as Solix's body swelled until she almost seemed to fill the cave, a huge, monstrous, bloated shape. Her bulbous eyes shone with hate. *She's stronger than ever!* Tom realised. *We have to stop more ants joining her!*

"Elenna," Tom called, "use your torch!"

"Good plan!" Elenna cried. She turned to Orla, still crouched against the cave wall. "Stay here," she said. Then she lifted her torch

and raced towards a crack, where
a steady stream of tiny bodies was
entering the cave. Elenna bent
and lowered her torch. She swept
it across the opening, creating a
long arc of crackling orange flame.
The tide of ants retreated as the
shadows leapt and swayed.

"It's working!" Elenna called,
racing to the next crack with her
torch.

Solix's head snapped around.
Her giant body turned, and a low,
menacing hiss echoed off the cavern
walls. Her jaws clashed together
as the light from Elenna's torch
reflected in her eyes. Tom heart
jolted painfully. Solix was crouched

like a coiled spring, all her deadly rage and power focussed on his friend. *I have to protect Elenna!*

Tom raced across the cavern floor and darted between the Beast's front legs, then lifted his sword and stabbed upwards.

A terrific gasp of agony filled the cave. Tom tugged his blade from Solix's shell and dived towards Elenna. Just as he passed from under the Beast's vast abdomen, one of her spiny front legs flicked towards him. His ribs exploded with pain as the blow connected, and he found himself hurtling through the gloom towards the cavern wall.

Blinding white light filled his

vision, then darkness swept over him. And silence.

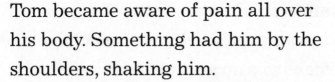

Tom became aware of pain all over his body. Something had him by the shoulders, shaking him.

"Tom! Wake up!" Elenna's voice was taut with fear.

Tom forced his heavy lids to open and saw her blurry outline. He blinked, focussing his eyes, and heard her breathe a sigh of relief.

"Tom, are you all right?" she asked. "When I saw your head hit that wall…" Elenna grimaced.

Tom pushed himself up to sitting. A wave of dizziness took hold of him.

He took a deep breath, letting it pass.

"I'm fine," he said, glancing about the cave. Orla stood in a halo of orange light behind Elenna, holding the torch above her head. The rest of the cave was murky with shadows. There was no sign of the Beast.

"Where's Solix?" Tom asked.

Elenna pointed to a low, black gash in the rock at the back of the cave. "She was wounded by your blow, Elenna said. "She crawled away through that tunnel."

She must be able to change shape as well as heal herself… Tom thought.

He picked up his sword and shield, and pushed himself slowly to his feet. The cave spun sickeningly around him, but Tom focussed his eyes, and started towards the tunnel. "We'd better get in there after her," he said.

"But what are we going to do when we find her?" Elenna said. "She's invincible."

Tom shook his head. "No Beast is invincible. Remember, Solix is nothing more than an evil spell created from innocent jungle creatures. I'm going to break that spell. I'm going to free those ants and Orla's people from Kensa's magic."

SOLIX'S LAIR

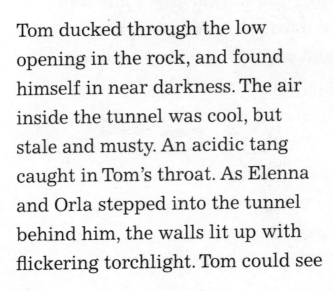

Tom ducked through the low opening in the rock, and found himself in near darkness. The air inside the tunnel was cool, but stale and musty. An acidic tang caught in Tom's throat. As Elenna and Orla stepped into the tunnel behind him, the walls lit up with flickering torchlight. Tom could see the floor was smooth and even, as if it had been worn away by many years of use, and it sloped steeply downwards.

"Stay ready," said Tom, holding out his sword. They descended. Orla's wavering flame only lit a few paces ahead. Tom strained his eyes into the gloom for any sign of movement. The path went on and on, until the bright colours and sounds of the Rainbow Jungle seemed like a half-forgotten dream.

Finally, Tom could see a yawning maw of blackness ahead that Orla's torchlight didn't touch. *Another cave.* He stopped.

The lair of the Beast.

"I'll go first," Elenna whispered.

"No!" Tom hissed. "It's too dangerous. You can't use your bow in this darkness."

"I know," Elenna said, "but I can distract Solix. You watch and wait for the right moment, then strike. The Beast must have a weak point, somewhere on her body. If we inflict enough damage, she might not be able to re-form."

Tom shook his head, his jaw clenched. The idea of sending Elenna ahead of him into danger… *How can I let her take that chance?* But Elenna was watching him steadily, her eyes shining in the torchlight – calm and unafraid. Tom could see that she trusted herself – and she trusted him.

"All right," Tom said. "But take my sword for protection. Get Solix to fight you, and I will look for her weakness. Orla – Solix won't attack you if you hold that torch. Keep it steady. Without its light, we're doomed."

Orla nodded, her eyes wide and solemn.

Elenna held Tom's sword before her face. "Let's go!" she said.

Tom stood at Orla's side, close behind Elenna as she stepped into the cave. The space opened up around them, swallowing the light from their torch. The cavern was vast – high walls reaching up into blackness. The floor was of hard-packed earth, crumbling beneath Tom's feet.

Elenna took a few steps further into the cave, brandishing the blade. Tom heard a series of sharp clicks. Then the light from Orla's torch glanced off something huge and hideous at the back of the cavern. A bulbous, shining head... Two inky

teardrop eyes… Long, shining legs and razor-sharp jaws.

Tom had to hold himself back, swallowing his instinct to charge. Orla gripped hold of his sleeve. Even through the fabric, Tom could feel her shaking.

"Yah!" Elenna raced across the cave floor, straight towards the Beast, swinging Tom's sword with two hands. Solix pounced forwards at the same moment, her jointed legs glinting in the torchlight as she sprang towards Elenna.

The sword smashed into Solix's jaws, leaving a gash in her shell. The Beast let out a vicious hiss of rage, and her bulbous abdomen whipped around, its pointed sting jabbing for Elenna's chest. Tom wanted to rush in, but Elenna leapt back and slashed the sword across the tip of Solix's deadly sting. The Beast drew back her tail, jaws rattling in rage. Tom shifted round the cavern

as he watched from the shadows,
waiting for his chance. Elenna
lunged and swiped again, her sword
scoring a deep cut in Solix's foreleg.
The Beast's spiked jaws snapped

towards her, but Elenna hopped sideways and spun. Her sword glinted as it smashed against the Beast's dark mandible. Solix's head jerked up, lifting her pincers out of range of Elenna's sharp blade.

Torchlight shimmered off the Beast's exposed underbelly. Tom saw his moment.

He turned to Orla. "Stay here," he hissed. Then he focussed his eyes on a single shining point between the Beast's jointed forelegs and called on the power of his golden breastplate, channelling its magical strength into the muscles of his arm and balling his fist....

Tom charged, drawing back his

arm and smashing his fist into the
Beast's weak point.

SMACK!

"Aargh!" Tom cried, reeling back,

cradling his aching hand.

Solix twitched, hunching in on herself and crouching low to the ground, her knees bent and her antennae flat against her head.

"Of course!" Orla cried. "Jungle ants hate noise. The elders used drums and fiddles to drive them away when there were too many in the village."

Tom glanced towards Solix. Her colossal body was uncurling slowly as the hollow echoes of his blow died away. Her feelers started to twitch.

Tom smiled. "So, the Beast doesn't like music," he said. "Well, in that case I think we have a plan. Elenna

– keep her busy. I'm going to make some noise."

TROUBLE ABOVE THE TREETOPS

Elenna squared her shoulders and lifted Tom's sword as the Beast scuttled around to face her. The creature's huge eyes glinted with menace. Tom tugged Ronak's horn from his belt. He had known that this was going to come in handy. Raising the sword, Elenna charged.

Solix's gigantic pincers snapped open, gaping wide.

Tom put his mouth to the horn and blew. No sound came out. Elenna brought the blade down hard on the black, armoured jaws reaching towards her. The sword glanced off, and the pincers sliced onwards. Elenna let out a strangled yelp as the jaws clamped shut around her waist.

Tom desperately tried to sound the horn again, but all that came out of it was air.

No!

Tom's sword fell from Elenna's grip and clattered to the ground as she was swept upwards.

Orla ran over to Tom, panting, her
eyes locked on the horn. "You have
to purse your lips, so they vibrate!
It's how the horn players do it in my
village."

Tom realised she was right. He
clenched his lips together, leaving

the smallest of gaps for the air to pass. He took a deep breath, his eyes on Elenna's kicking legs, dangling above him.

This has to work!

He blew into the horn. A deep, rich note filled the cave, growing in intensity as it reverberated off the walls. Solix froze, Elenna still clasped in her sharp mandibles. The Beast's body started to tremble. Tom could feel the vibration of the horn's note coming up through his boots. Every part of his body seemed to hum along with the sound. The cavern appeared to shudder, and dust and small stones skittered about on the floor.

Tom kept blowing, puffing out the air from his cheeks and drawing more in through his nose. As he sustained the note it grew, echoing back to him, gaining in power and volume. Orla clamped her hands

over her ears. Solix's legs started quivering uncontrollably. She shook her mighty head as if trying to block out the sound, whipping Elenna from side to side. Then finally, as Tom thought he could hold the note no longer, the Beast's jaws fell open, and Elenna tumbled free. She hit the ground in a crouch, and stumbled away to join Orla.

Tom took the horn from his lips and caught his breath. The dying note echoed around him. The Beast was shaking all over now, the rattle of her joints adding to the din. Her spindly legs buckled. Her head slumped. Then, with a long, rasping sigh, she crumpled slowly to the ground. Tom took a cautious step towards her, then another, crossing the cave floor to reach his fallen sword.

He hooked the toe of his boot under the hilt of his sword, and flicked it up, snatching it from the air. He aimed the tip of the blade right between the creature's eyes.

Solix's antennae twitched feebly.

It's time to end this...

Tom brought the horn to his lips once more, and blew a long, powerful note. As the sound swelled, a tiny crack appeared in the corner of Solix's eye socket. It spread, criss-crossing her shell, running across her back and down her legs.

The surface of her body seemed to blur, losing its sheen. Then all at once, the giant ant collapsed in on herself, her hard, shiny shell becoming an avalanche of tiny bodies and scrabbling legs.

There were ants everywhere, scrambling over each other, flowing

towards the entrance of the cave
where Orla and Elenna waited. For
a moment, Tom thought they were
attacking, but then the stream of
insects parted to flow around their
feet. Torchlight glinted off countless
shiny shells – no longer inky black,
but a glowing ruby red.

Tom let the note from the horn fade. He kept still as the river of blood-red ants streamed past his boots. As they raced along, something caught his eye on the cave floor. *Is that...?* Carefully crouching, Tom saw a pair of gloves made from rock-hard ant armour. He picked them up. *These look they'll be useful on a future Quest!* He stood back up and made his way carefully to Elenna and Orla.

"They're back to normal!" Orla said. She looked up at Tom, her eyes shining with joy.

Tom smiled. "Then let's find your people and get you home," he said.

He led Elenna and Orla back

up the steep tunnel, the flow of
ants parting around them as the
tiny creatures swarmed upwards
towards the cave above. Soon Tom
could see the faint, green light
of the jungle outlined by the low
entrance to the main cave. He
stepped through with Elenna and
Orla at his side, then crossed the
cavern.

When they passed out from
under the overhang, they stood
for a moment, watching the river
of insects break up into smaller
streams, and eventually single lines
of red ants, marching steadily away
through the trees.

"Orla!" a man's voice cried from

the undergrowth, raw with emotion.

Orla turned and raced towards the sound. "Father!" she shouted.

A thickset man dressed in a russet tunic stepped from the shadows.

Orla leapt into his open arms, and he swung her around, covering her head with kisses.

"You're safe!" he said, setting Orla back on the ground. "We've been so worried. The rest of the villagers are deep in the jungle. When we heard a horn blowing, I came to find out what it meant. Then I saw that the ants were red again. And here you are! All of our prayers have been answered at once. Your mother will be so relieved!"

"It's all thanks to Tom and Elenna," Orla said, turning towards them. "They healed me when I was sick, and defeated a giant ant monster with a magic horn."

Orla's father dipped his head towards Tom and Elenna in gratitude. Tom stepped forwards, holding out his hand. The man shook it heartily, then Elenna's.

"It sounds like there is a long story to tell here," Orla's father said, "and much to be grateful for. We are in your debt. Thanks to you, maybe now things can get back to normal. It won't be easy, especially if those pirates keep coming back, but we've faced challenges before."

Tom felt his fists clench. "I hope we run into Sanpao's crew on the way to Jengtor," he said. "It's about time they found out what happens to thieves and bullies!"

Elenna gasped suddenly, and pointed upwards. "I think we're going to get our chance sooner than we'd expected!"

Tom followed the line of her finger. Through the bright gaps in the tree canopy, he could just make out the underside of a curved timber hull and the swell of billowing white sails.

He turned to Orla and her father. "I'm afraid it's time for us to bid you farewell," he said. "We have a pirate ship to catch!" He stuffed the ant armour gloves into his tunic. Then he nodded to Elenna. "Let's get after them!"

9

TAKING FLIGHT

Tom raced through the
undergrowth, leaping roots and
ducking between ferns and vines
with Elenna close behind him. Soon
they were at the jungle's outskirts,
near where they had first entered.
High above, Sanpao's pirate ship
was descending fast, sailing towards
the edge of the jungle. Tom could

hear it ploughing through the tree canopy ahead, smashing branches, sending brightly coloured birds squawking from their perches. Then Tom heard a panicked whinny from beyond the treeline.

"They're going to steal our horses!" Elenna cried.

"Not while there's blood in my veins!" Tom vowed.

He and Elenna plunged onwards, gasping for breath in the sweltering heat. Finally, they burst from the edge of the jungle into open grassland.

The pirate ship was hanging low over the plain. Two men, bare-chested and covered in tattoos, were

already on the ground, wrestling
Storm and Angel into harnesses
attached to ropes. Aboard the
ship, teams of pirates held tight to
winches ready to pull the horses up.

Sanpao leaned from the prow,
a satisfied grin spread over his
tattooed face. The pirates on the
ground leapt onto the struggling
horses' backs. Tom drew his sword
and sprinted across the plain
towards them.

"Leave those horses alone!" he
cried.

"Too late!" Sanpao shouted. He
lifted his hand, gesturing to the
pirates behind him. "Heave!"

The pirates on board hauled on

their winches, and the horses started to rise, hooves dangling and eyes rolling with fear. The pirates sitting on the horses' backs leered down at Tom as he raced towards them. But it was hopeless. When he reached the spot where the horses had been, they were far above his head. Elenna arrived at his side, panting, and looked up at the terrified mares.

"How are you going to get to Jengtor now, eh?" Sanpao shouted down to them.

"We'll get there!" Tom called back, "And when we do, I'll make you pay for what you've done!" But Tom's words rang hollowly in his own ears.

Sanpao spat, then let out a long,

throaty chuckle. "Turn her about,
lads," he barked to the pirates behind
him. "Set a course for Jengtor!"

Tom and Elenna watched
helplessly as Angel and Star rose
higher. Once the horses crested the
gunwale, the pirates tugged them

roughly aboard, and the ship started to turn back towards the Rainbow Jungle.

Tom's heart sank. *If we don't reach Jengtor soon, people will die. My mother will die!*

"We can't let them get away!" Elenna cried. She pulled her bow from her back, and aimed an arrow up at the ship.

"Don't shoot!" Tom said. "You'll just send them away quicker, and we need to get those horses."

"But how?" Elenna said.

Tom looked her in the eye, a plan forming in his mind. "Do you trust me?" he asked.

"Of course," she said. "Why?"

"Because I'm going to give you a boost!'

Elenna's eyebrows shot upwards and her mouth dropped open as Tom knelt and cupped his hands. She turned her face up towards Sanpao's ship, then back to Tom. She was deathly pale.

"All right," she said, finally. "Let's do it." She placed her foot into Tom's waiting hands.

Tom called on the magic of his golden breastplate, drew a deep breath, and hurled her skywards.

Elenna flew as straight and fast as an arrow fired from her bow, her arms raised towards the ship above.

Tom held his breath, watching

his friend soar higher and higher.
The nearer to the ship she climbed
the slower she went. Tom's stomach
lurched. She was still some distance
from the ship, but she was losing
momentum.

She has to make it!

Elenna's arms stretched out before her, reaching towards the figurehead at the prow of the ship. Her fingers opened, grasping for it...

Please...

Yes! Elenna clamped both hands around the neck of the carved Beast skull and clung on. Tom let out his breath, lightheaded with relief. Then he called on the power of his golden boots, took a long stride, bent his knees and launched himself after her.

The wind whipped at his face as he sprang upwards towards the pirate ship. The sails were full and it was picking up speed, moving towards him as he flew.

The figurehead surged closer. He reached out his hands. He had to catch hold of Elenna or he'd hit the hull of the ship! Her boots were right before him. He wrapped his arms around her ankles and clung on.

Elenna gasped at the sudden weight. Tom looked up to see her face already turning pink with the strain of supporting them both. He glanced down. The Rainbow Jungle was spread out below them, a patchwork of greens and browns, cut through with glittering silver streams. Wisps of cloud curled around him, cold and wet on his face, but when he looked up, he could see beads of sweat on Elenna's forehead. Her teeth were clenched and her eyes were wide with panic.

"Hold on, Elenna!" Tom called up to her.

"I'm trying!" she gasped through clenched jaws.

We can't fall, Tom thought. *If we do, there will be no one left to save Gwildor!*

Tom reached forward to grab the edge of the ship's Beast-skull figurehead, harnessing the power of his golden breastplate to haul himself up. He peered over the gunwale, seeing that the coast was clear. He reached down to take Elenna by the wrist and help her clamber up and over onto the deck, before scrambling over himself.

The two friends hid, breathless,
behind two stacked treasure chests.
Sanpao was bellowing orders. "Make

for the capital… Make for Jengtor!"

Tom saw Elenna grinning at him. "We've got the element of surprise," she said.

He nodded back at her. "There is no way he will storm the Emperor's palace…not while there's blood in my veins. Our Quest continues!"

CONGRATULATIONS, YOU HAVE COMPLETED THIS QUEST!

At the end of each chapter you were awarded a special gold coin.
The QUEST in this book was worth an amazing 9 coins.

Look at the Beast Quest totem picture inside the back cover of this book to see how far you've come in your journey to become

MASTER OF THE BEASTS.

The more books you read, the more coins you will collect!

Do you want your own
Beast Quest Totem?

1. Cut out and collect the coin below
2. Go to the Beast Quest website
3. Download and print out your totem
4. Add your coin to the totem
www.beastquest.co.uk/totem

Don't miss the next exciting Beast Quest book, KANIS THE SHADOW HOUND!

Read on for a sneak peek...

CHAPTER ONE

SNAKE EYES

Tom crouched next to Elenna, hiding behind a cluster of barrels on the deck of Sanpao's flying ship. Safe! *Except now we're stuck*

hundreds of feet up in the air with a crew of bloodthirsty pirates who might spot us at any moment...
Peering over the barrels, Tom saw that the deck was bustling. Sanpao's pirates were swarming up and down the rigging, swabbing the decks and adjusting the sails. They wore garish silks and satins and clattered with weaponry – cutlasses, axes, clubs... Tom spotted the captain himself swinging in a hammock strung up between two masts, bellowing orders in between taking swigs from a flask.

"Stir your stumps, lads! Tie down those kegs, and look sharp about it!" Tom felt a flicker of rage at the sight of his old enemy, with his greasy black ponytail, yellowing teeth and fading tattoos. Sanpao had done wicked things in the past, but this time he and the witch Kensa had poisoned Tom's own mother. And while Freya lay sick in Jengtor, the capital of Gwildor, Sanpao and Kensa were making plans to capture the city for themselves.

Tom gritted his teeth. *We're lucky the Good Witch Irina can protect Jengtor with her magic, because otherwise—*

"Look," whispered Elenna, interrupting Tom's thoughts. She was pointing to the far side of the deck. Tom followed her finger and saw their horses Angel and Star tied up.

Star spotted them and let out a hopeful whicker.

"Shh," Tom soothed the horse. Then with one swift movement he vaulted the barrels and crouched down behind a giant coil of rope. Elenna followed, landing softly next to him.

"There's something weird going on here," Elenna whispered.

Read *Kanis the Shadow Hound* to find out what happens next!

Discover the new Beast Quest mobile game from

Available free on iOS and Android

Available on **iTunes**   GET IT ON **Google play**   **amazon**.com

Guide Tom on his Quest to free the Good Beasts
of Avantia from Malvel's evil spells.

Battle the Beas
unearth the sec
rewards as you
Kingdom of Ava

DOWNLOAD THE A
THE ADVENTU